A WORLD OF MANY WARS

By J. W. Criniti

CONTENTS

INTRODUCTION

Throughout the early 1900s, there were many immigrants of all nationalities, races, and creeds, emigrating from all over the world to the United States in search for a better life. America was the land of opportunity, and although it must have been an absolutely terrifying journey to make, with so many factors unknown, they did it just the same and were extremely grateful for the chance to become U.S. citizens. These immigrants built our bridges, reached for the skylines with our tallest buildings, and helped shape the nation we are today. Included in those immigrants which many people seem to forget about are Japanese-Americans. Due to the terrible acts committed by the Japanese government to launch World War II, many people forget that we had Japanese in our country before the war who greatly contributed to the success of our nation. But after the devasting attacks on Pearl Harbor in Hawaii that launched the United States into its Second World War, President Roosevelt made the extremely difficult and controversial decision to open up internment camps for Japanese Americans. It was feared that they had the potential of being spies or invaders. While I'm not defending the decision by any means, the thought process is understandable. We were just completely blind-sided by the Japanese after months of promised peace during diplomatic talks. It all ended up being a charade to set up one of the most infamous and successful sneak attacks in the history of modern warfare. It's an extremely unfortunate black eye to the history of our great nation that we treated our own citizens with such contempt. Many families were separated during these times and weren't reunited until after the war. Many, were never reunited again. History is always written by the victors and it always seems that this important fact is left out of many history books or briefly overlooked. This fictional story will be depicted from a totally different point of view of the war and the different struggles faced over the course of that time period. Although the characters and specific events may be fictional, make no mistake, there are real people who experienced the war in this light. The goal of this book is to bring a widely unknown perspective of the greatest victory in our country's history since winning our independence from the British. Buckle up and follow the greatest generation through their eventual triumph over the Axis Powers in pursuit of one of the all-time impressive military victories in history.

SUMMER 1941

It was a warm summer day in Oahu, Hawaii, home of the entirety of the U.S. Navy's pacific fleet. Haze gray ships littered Pearl Harbor as far as the eye could see. A war raged on across the vast Pacific Ocean in the skies above London and other European countries. Hitler's rabid army sank its teeth into entire nations as the blitzkrieg paved a road of blood across the heart of the continent. At the moment the U.S. remained neutral. We supplied our allies with weapons of war, but the general sentiment of the American people remained that we did not want to get involved in the affairs of Europe. After all, we had just won our independence from the Brits a little over 150 years earlier, but we did what we could to aid our older sibling in their war effort against Hitler. The truth of the matter was, our fleet was aging and all the years of isolationism had tremendously hurt our military effectiveness since the end of the Great War. It was very easy for the American public to turn a blind eye to the carnage and debris strewn across Europe when we ourselves had no dog in the fight. It would take a direct sucker-punch to the face to light a fire under the American people and the government in order for us to get our asses in gear and get into the fight. Little did we know, throughout the ongoing peace negotiations with Japan that were underway, they were clenching their fist and winding up to deliver just that. Jimmy Katsumoto rolled out of his rack on the USS Arizona on a sleepy summer morning. Jimmy was a second generation Japanese-American who also happened to be enlisted in the U.S. Navy as a Gunner's Mate Second Class. He was 20 years old and had enlisted in the Navy right after high school two years before. He had no idea what would be in store for him over the 4-year enlistment he had signed, but was proud to be able to support the country he was born and raised in. Jimmy loved being an American and grew up in Southern California where a lot of Japanese immigrants called home in the 20s and 30s, just as his parents did. His father worked in a shipyard as a tradesman and his mother taught 3rd grade at the local elementary school. They both worked hard and even though they faced their own struggles as immigrants in the early days, fit into the American way of life and ideals perfectly. Jimmy and his younger sister Sarah grew up just like any other American kid would. They both loved baseball courtesy of their father being one of the biggest Brooklyn Dodger fans on the West Coast. Jimmy played throughout his childhood and into his high school years. He was the best shortstop in town and even got offers to play in college. He couldn't afford tuition and elected to join the navy and learn a skill instead. All of that lead him to this lazy Sunday morning onboard the USS Arizona. One eerily similar to a Sunday that was to come in the near future and be etched in the annals of history forever. But today was like any other weekend day in the Navy. He awoke to shower and shave and head out for liberty. Jimmy got ready and headed out onto the weather deck toward the brow where he could disembark the Arizona. He stood at the top step facing the Ensign flying magnificently over the great warship and snapped to attention. This was customary for sailors who were disembarking their ship for shore but were in civilian clothes. If he had been in uniform, he would have snapped to attention and delivered a crisp salute before making his way down the brow toward a weekend of drinking and fun out in town with his buddies. Jimmy didn't have a car yet but it was on his short list of things to do and fast. If he was ever going to impress any of the girls out in own, he would have to have a set of wheels to get from beach to bar and back again. He made it a point that with his next meager paycheck he would take his savings and go looking for an old heap at a cheap price that he could fix up when he wasn't out to sea or at work. As he hit the pier, his two buddies Tom Seaton and Ralph Mazarra were cruising by in Tom's brand-new 1940 Plymouth coupe. Tom came from a rather wealthy family, and his old man had got him the car as a high school graduation present. Jimmy always envied him for that car and hoped to have something similar someday. "You just wait until I get my set of wheels Tom!" Jimmy yelled. "Ya, ya shut up and get your ass in the back." Tom hollered back at Jimmy. The boys headed into town looking for the nearest bar with the coldest beer and the friendliest women. Their first stop of the day before hitting the beach was the regular hangout spot for sailors stationed at Pearl. It was a beach side bar called “The Shack”. The three eager guys were hoping to meet some female friends that wanted to tag along for the day. Sometimes they struck out, but today, little did they know, they would hit one out of the park. They strolled into the bar as cool as they possibly could. It was around 1 in the afternoon so the crowd was starting to get pretty big. They all took seats at the bar and ordered a beer a piece to get the day started. That’s when a beautiful long-haired brunette caught Jimmy’s eye from across the room. She was the most gorgeous girl he had ever laid eyes upon. She looked to be dressed for a beach trip as she stood near a table and gossiped with her two other friends. “I gotta find out her name” Jimmy thought to himself. He nudged Ralph’s arm who was totally oblivious to the situation. “Look over there man.” “Those three girls standing by the table over there. Let’s be smooth and see if they want out at the beach with us today.” Ralph wasn’t the smoothest with the ladies but Jimmy and Tom could hold their own. “You just keep quiet Ralphie and let us do the talking.” Tom squawked. After they had all gotten their beers, they each took a few generous swigs to gather up some more courage and smoothness to head over and talk to the pretty girls. “Here goes nothing!” Jimmy said enthusiastically as the three of them headed over to the table. The brunette that Jimmy was pining over was Cindy Jacobsen. She was a Navy brat and her father just so happened to be a one-star Admiral. Her two friends were Sharon and Kelly. But all Jimmy cared about was getting to know Cindy and getting her attention. Tom and Ralph could fight over the other two's attention and sort it out amongst themselves. "Hi ladies, I'm Tom this is Jimmy and Ralph and we couldn't help but notice that it looked like you guys were heading to the beach today. We were thinking of doing the same but we've got a pretty awesome secret spot we found a couple months back. Care to join us?" Tom said in his smoothest voice. The three of them looked pretty unimpressed at what we had to offer but Jimmy could tell they were interested in the made-up secret spot Tom had added in for good measure. Cindy seemed to speak for the whole group when she said "Where is this so-called secret spot you boys have?" as she called Tom's bluff. "Well it's classified." Tom said trying to sound important and mysterious. "But if you promise to keep it a secret, we will show you." The place Tom had in mind was on the west side of the island and wasn't necessarily a secret but it wasn't as well known as the rest of the beaches were in the area. It was a little bit of a hike to get there but it was worth it in the end. The girls seemed intrigued and agreed to tag along. They all spent the next hour or so getting acquainted at the bar before they hit the road toward the west side of the island. Jimmy was doing his damnedest to get Cindy's attention but it didn't seem to be working. She seemed more interested in Tom from the start. It may be some work but he'd have to do something to get her attention off of Tom, or he would be in for a long hot day in the sun. The brakes of Tom's Plymouth squeaked as they pulled up to the secret beach. The girls had tagged along in their own car, a beautiful Cadillac that was most likely owned by one of their parents. Everyone jumped out of both cars and in a dead sprint, headed for the water and jumped in. The rest of the day was filled with laughter and horseplay as the sun made its way to sleep. The sunset that evening was something out of a picture book. Oranges, yellows, and reds kissed the horizon and illuminated the clouds left over from the daytime. They all sat around a campfire that Jimmy had made a few minutes before and admired nature's true beauty. "This has to be the most beautiful place on God's earth." Cindy said in awe of the view. "I'm really glad we decided to tag along with you guys. I don't think I've ever seen a sunset this beautiful in all my time here." She proclaimed. Jimmy knew this was his chance to grab her attention. "If you think this view is amazing, follow me." He gestured up towards a cliff overlooking the beach and the ocean. They both made their way up towards the top of the Blough. At that moment, Tom knew Jimmy had her. He wasn't at all mad because he knew Jimmy had interest in her from the beginning and that's what good friends do. As Cindy and

Jimmy reached the top of the cliff, she was awe-struck. The view truly felt as if you could reach out and grab the cotton-candy clouds. The reflection off the uncharacteristically calm water looked like God had laid down a mirror on top of the ocean, and the sunset was duplicated almost perfectly. "I absolutely love sunsets." Cindy said. "They are the fastest way to my heart. Are you trying to impress me Jimmy?" she said playfully. "No ma'am. I just figured that eyes as beautiful as yours would truly appreciate the beauty nature has to offer." Jimmy said smoothly. She gave him a little smirk and they both continued to admire the sky as the sun disappeared completely. They headed back down to the fire and their friends. Ralph had broken out the guitar and was playing some tunes around the fire. Little did Cindy and Jimmy know, but they were absolutely hooked on each other. Things would get complicated in the coming future. But that summer night could've lasted forever. When morning broke on the beach, the sun kissed all of their sleepy faces. Everyone had either passed out right on the beach or crawled into the backseat of the cars. Jimmy woke up with Cindy nestled onto his arm and he couldn't have had a bigger smile. They headed back into town and the two groups spent the rest of the weekend together drinking and having a great time. When Monday came it was time to report back to the ship. None of them wanted the weekend to end, but all promised to get together again as soon as they possibly could. Cindy and

Jimmy weren't the only young romance to blossom out of the two groups getting together. Tom ended up seeing Sharon and Ralph briefly dated Kelly. The rest of the summer was spent on the beach or in the bars. It would be one of the last calm relaxing moments all of them would see for the next 4 years. Trouble was brewing in the South Pacific and Japan was eventually going to wake the sleeping isolationist giant that was the United States of America.

FALL 1941

Summer had been chased away by fall, although in Hawaii, the only thing that truly changed were the months. The weather remained as beautiful as ever, but the ever-changing landscape of the world hadn't. Turmoil in Europe raged on in solidarity with the Nazi war machine. The U.S. was still heavily involved in supply aspects only, providing war materials to our Allies to help them combat what seemed to be an all-out rush to take over Europe by the Nazis. President Roosevelt did his best to keep American interest strictly in America, at the wishes of the isolationist population of the time. Although that task became increasingly difficult with each passing day. There was however, a light at the end of the tunnel for the United States it seemed, as peace talks with Japan continued to progress. It was apparent that neither of the countries wished to go to war with each other, or so it seemed at the time. Everyday life hadn't changed all that much for the men stationed in sleepy Pearl Harbor. They continued their duties on the ship, going underway for training as required. It was a stormy day in October on board the USS Arizona, who was underway off the coast of Hawaii conducting live-fire exercises. Jimmy, Tom, and Ralph were all stationed aboard the Arizona together, making their friendship more of a brotherhood, only understood by those who have been out to sea on a Navy Vessel. Jimmy and Tom were both Gunner's Mate Second Classes while Ralph was a Boatswain's Mate Third Class. He got his fair share of shit talking from Jimmy and Tom, as there was a healthy rivalry between the deck department and the weapons division. Both of them out-ranking Ralph usually meant he got the shit end of the stick, but it was always in good fun. Jimmy and Tom were part of Arizona's 14-inch gun crew. An imperative part of the ship's offensive and defensive capabilities. Arizona carried twelve 14-inch 45 caliber guns separated into turrets I-IV from forward to aft of the ship. Jimmy and Tom were both part of Turret number II. Each in charge of their own barrel. There was always a friendly rivalry between Jimmy and Tom for who could get their gun ready to fire faster and keep their machinery cleaner. The Navy always brings out the competitive spirit in most. This particular underway was dragging out longer than usual. Typically, they'd head out, complete their live-fire exercises and get the hell back to port. But the Skipper kept running through the drills over and over again. A lot more than they ever had before. Everyone could sense the seriousness in the drills so they did their best to be efficient, safe and accurate. Maybe things with Japan weren't going as well as they'd originally been portrayed by the government. Nonetheless, Jimmy and Tom both wanted to get back to port to see their sweethearts. Jimmy couldn't stop thinking about Cindy. In the months since their spontaneous beach trip, things had gotten fairly serious and they were going steady. She was the first person he ran off the ship to at the end of a long work day. Something about her calmed him and made a stressful day melt away. They were young, but they were definitely serious about each other. "Man, I can't wait till the old man takes us back to port so I can get my ass off this rusting hulk." Jimmy said to Tom during cleaning stations as he nodded in agreement. Cleaning stations was an integral part of the daily life of a sailor. It was an hour in the morning and afternoon where work on the ship ceased and everyone cleaned their designated areas. For the Gunner's Mates, it was a point of pride. They took this time to polish all the brass in their compartments so well that you could see a perfect reflection in them as you walked by. This was another point of competition between Jimmy and Tom. They'd have contest to see who could get their brass polished better and have them judged by a stranger walking by. That was Navy life as boring as it sounded. But in peace-time there wasn't a whole lot to do other than practice for being at war. Nobody knew exactly what lay ahead for the crew of the Arizona, but many suspected that the U.S. would soon be a hell of a lot more involved in the ongoing conflict in the world than they currently were. That was just fine for most of them. The day to day ship life was getting boring, and many of them wanted to see action and get their chance to whoop some ass and see what the Arizona could really do. Ralph strutted over to Jimmy and Tom towards the end of cleaning stations to talk his usual shit to them about their cleaning and polishing skills. "You call that brass polished? I've seen cleaner brass on the underside of a shitter!" Ralph snickered. Jimmy and Tom smiled at each other as they made their way towards Ralph. "Well in that case let us show you the underside of the shitter we just cleaned!" Jimmy howled as they both grabbed Ralph and pretended to drag him to the nearest head, much like high school bullies would the class nerd for a swirly. It was all in good fun. You have to do something to pass the time while out to sea. If you don't horse around a little, you will go absolutely nuts. The Boatswain piped the end of cleaning stations over the 1MC, or the ships intercom system. It was just about time to head down to the galley for chow before another round of live-fire exercises that afternoon. Word around the ship was, after today's training, the old man was final going to turn the big broad towards Oahu and bring our sorry asses into port for a much-needed liberty weekend. Rumors like that always flowed around the ship towards the end of an underway. It was just like high-school and sometimes worse. Jimmy, Tom, and Ralph stood in the chow line to get their daily serving of "Slop" as they called it. The food on Navy ships was never the greatest, but it could always be much worse. They could be eating C-rations that grunts in the field have to eat. They contained much worse food than anything served on a ship, so they were sort of half-assed thankful for the "Slop" they ate every day. As they all grabbed seats in the galley, Jimmy couldn't help but notice a table of guys glaring at him. As he walked by, he couldn't quite hear what they were whispering but he swore he heard Cindy's name come out of one of their mouths. He brushed it off and assumed that they had seen the two of them together at the bar, and were jealous that he had a beautiful girlfriend. Not out of the norm for life on board a ship. Chances were, more people than you thought, knew a lot about you. The glare continued throughout chow and Jimmy began to get irritated. "Those clowns over there can't stop looking over here at me and talking shit. I heard them say something about Cindy when we walked by." Jimmy said visibly heated. Tom had a slight smirk and knew this probably wasn't the time to egg him on, but he couldn't help himself. "Well why don't you stroll over there and take a seat with those gentlemen and find out just what they think is so funny." Tom said smartly. "That's the only way you're going to find out." He declared. Jimmy thought to himself "Maybe I can turn this into a joke and make these idiots look and feel stupid." When he finished his food he got up to throw out his trash and turn his tray into the Scullery or dishwashing room. On his way back to the table he changed course and grabbed an empty seat at the table of the 3 guys who had been glaring at him, much to their surprise. "How's it going today fellas?" Jimmy said smartly "Is there anything I can help you with? I noticed you guys have been staring at me for quite some time and I was just wondering if you thought I was pretty or something." Jimmy said with sarcasm. This ticked off the main guy in the group who happened to work in the deck department. "Well, boy, we just couldn't figure out how a squinty eyed Jap like you pulled such a beautiful girlfriend. Surely, she knows we are about to be at war with your homeland. Maybe then she will get a real American Man like me." He said confidently. Jimmy could feel the fire burning in his belly and the sweat beginning to form on his brow. How they hell could they claim he wasn't an American man? He was right alongside them serving in the same military as them for the country he loved and respected so deeply. Hell, he was born on American soil just like them. Maybe he looked a little different, but his ties to the country were just as strong. They both stood up fists clenched ready to throw down. "Why don't you put your money where your mouth is tough guy." Jimmy Challenged. "I'll show you who the hell is a real American when I kick your ass in front of all your friends." He declared. By this time Tom and Ralph had jumped up to separate the scrum. Ralph worked with the guy causing the problems who went by the name of Dick Tripton so he did his best to de-escalate the situation. Tom grabbed Jimmy and convinced him to save it for Liberty. "You know if you beat his ass now, the old man will put you in the brig and you'll miss liberty this weekend. Save it for out in town. We will get him what he's got coming to him buddy don't you worry." Tom reassured Jimmy. "See you out in town this weekend Dick." Jimmy threatened as they all headed out of the galley and back to work. There was always something eventful happening on board the Arizona, you could definitely count on that. That afternoon's training exercises came and went as scheduled. Before evening prayer, which was when the chaplain came over the 1MC to pray with the entire ship just before Taps and lights out, the Skipper came on and confirmed the rumors swirling about the ship. "Okay shipmates, it's come to my attention that rumor around the ship has us steaming toward port tomorrow morning bright and early. I'm here to tell you that isn't true. We've actually already begun to steam home and should be pier side before noon!" The Skipper said with as much excitement as you'd ever get out of him. Everyone in the berthing cheered from their bunks. It was always an event when they were finally heading home. Even if they had only been out a few weeks. All Jimmy could think of as he laid in his rack was Cindy jumping into his arms and taking her to the beach to spend some quality alone time with her. He was young but he was falling for her like crazy. He wasn't even sure if he knew what that meant but he didn't care. She was his girl and he wanted to tell the whole entire world. So, he screamed it in the berthing "I can't fucking wait to see my girl!" Jimmy yelled. A chorus of "Nobody cares asshole, go to sleep." Came echoing back from just about the entire berthing. Jimmy couldn't help but grin as he rolled over to finally try and grab some rest. His mind drifted off into the future, thinking of what life could possibly be like. He didn't even think of the war that could bear down on the United States at any moment. His mind was somewhere else entirely for the first time in a while. He let some of the stress and weight of what he was doing melt off. In a short while, he was sound asleep. Reveille came quick and before Jimmy knew it, the Boatswains mate was piping it over the 1MC and telling everyone to heave out and trice up. The voice was extremely familiar. Ralph! He must have pulled piping duty that morning, meaning he had to wake up extra early. He would remember to bust his balls about it later for sounding like a 12-year-old boy over the 1MC. Jimmy hopped out of his rack and tidied everything up. The last thing he wanted was an ass- chewing for a messy rack before liberty later that day. He walked to the head to grab a fresh shave and get ready for the day of waiting around to get off that old broad and get to Cindy. He glided through the passage ways toward his turret to get everything ship shape for pulling into port. While on his way, he passed none other than Dick Tripton. They made eye contact and Jimmy couldn't help but say "Catch you out there this weekend asshole." Dick smirked and said "I look forward to it you Jap bastard." Jimmy knew he'd be getting into a pretty good brawl at some point that weekend if he saw Dick but he didn't give a damn. He was going to stand up for himself and for his family's honor. Hopefully Tom and Ralph would be around to back him up in case things got crazy. The three of them wearily ambled off the brow after their crisp salute of the ensign, toward the sweet release of solid land and a cold beer. Both of which they hadn't had the pleasure of experiencing for almost a month. Life in the Navy wasn't terrible, but it was times like these after an underway period that many sailors truly grew to appreciate the simple things in life. Like a cold mug of beer and a fresh meal not cooked by a disgruntled cook below decks on a U.S. Navy vessel. The guys jumped into Tom's car that was parked out past the pier where the Arizona normally berthed. They were off to the usual post-underway bar spot "The Shack". The same bar and grill they had met Cindy and the girls at the previous summer. It wasn't much, but they had made it their hangout ever since they got stationed on the island. It was a ritual to go before and after a successful underway. On the way over, Jimmy, Tom, and Ralph talked about the normal things guys in their late teens early twenties talked about. Girls, baseball, cars, and girls. "Boy, I really need to get my own set of wheels. I'm tired of riding in your heap of junk, Tom." Jimmy said laughingly. "Well I can drop your skinny ass off right here and you can walk to The Shack from here if you'd like! Only about 5 miles, you should make it there just after I'm finishing my third beer and dancing with your girl!" Tom said playfully. "I'm seriously going to start looking for something soon. I need something to keep me busy. I'm tired of only polishing brass and turning wrenches for the Navy." Jimmy said with a serious tone. "We will get you hooked up with something nice. But first we need some hydration and to calm our weary minds in the presence of some beautiful women." Tom exclaimed. As they rolled up to the bar, it seemed relatively dead for a Friday after a battleship had just pulled into port. It was the end of November and they had been out to sea for Thanksgiving, so everyone was kind of hoping for a big get-together at The Shack with all the regulars to make up for missing the holiday. As the guys walked inside, they found the girls sitting at a table waiting patiently for them. "If those aren't some sorry looking sailors!" Cindy said affectionately as she ran into Jimmy's arms. "I hope you boys behaved yourself out there." Sharon said as she gave Tom a hug and a kiss. "Mostly, other than Jimmy almost getting in a galley-brawl with some knucklehead." Ralph said. Both Jimmy and Tom glared at Ralph as if he shouldn't have brought it up. "It was nothing I can't handle." Jimmy reassured Cindy. Truthfully, Jimmy knew there would be more trouble that weekend if he came across Dick Tripton, and it just so happened he also frequented The Shack regularly with his gang of friends. For the sake of a pleasant and rather uneventful weekend, Jimmy was hoping that they wouldn't pay their usual visit. Just as that thought crossed his mind, none other than Dick himself came rudely barging through the door. Somehow already 3 sheets to the wind, even though they had just gotten off the ship only about an hour and a half earlier. Many guys liked to get a head start on drinking before leaving the ship, usually from private stashes in their bunks. Although completely against Navy policy, it was standard practice, and anyone of authority typically looked the other way for fear of having their own stash discovered. Dick had definitely come looking for trouble and despite the amount of alcohol he had consumed, he hadn't forgotten his parting shot at Jimmy as they both exited the ship. When he made eye contact with Jimmy, all he did was point at him and say "You! Asshole!" Jimmy looked at Ralph and Tom and leaned over the table to the girls "You Gals should probably head outside. We've gotta take care of a little problem and it may get messy." Jimmy said confidently. Cindy knew that look in his eye and took head to his warning. As the girls walked out of the bar she looked back with worry in her eyes "Please be careful Jimmy." She said tenderly. Within a split second the two groups of guys were nose to nose. It was hard to tell who started swinging first, but in the blink of an eye an all out brawl was unfolding inside The Shack. The owner jumped over the counter to break it up "You all better take this shit outside before I call the cops and they toss your asses in the brig!" By the time the brawl made it outside everyone had got their licks in and some other sailors managed to break it up. Everyone came out with bumps and bruises and a couple bloody noses but it ended up being a relatively even contest. They all shouted their parting shots at each other after it was all over as was typically custom after a display of bravado and testosterone. Dick and his gang of buddies jumped into their cars and sped off into the afternoon. Cindy and the girls made their way towards their group of battered men who were recapping the fight and joking around. She was not happy with Jimmy at all. She, like most other mature and intelligent women, thought that fighting solved nothing and was childish. She looked over Jimmy with disapproval for any serious injuries. She happened to be interning at the Naval hospital on base while in school to become a Registered Nurse. "You guys are all a bunch of ridiculous jerks! It's pretty rude to get in a full-fledged childish brawl in front of your girlfriends!" She scowled. "Call me when you grow up a little. We are going to go have fun like adults." Cindy said as they made their way to her car. Jimmy knew he had to figure out a way to make it up to her, but first they had to drink off the head and body aches they all had. Looks like it was going to be a boy's night out instead. The beers flowed all night at several different bars across the island. Luckily, they never ran into Dick and his gang again, because undoubtedly there would have been a rematch of the earlier bout. It was around 2 in the morning when they decided to attempt to stumble back to the ship for some much-needed rest. There was an official curfew of around midnight, but the guys happened to be good friends with the sailors who stood the brow watch or the watch who allowed sailors access to the ship, so it was no issue if they were a couple hours late. Jimmy in particular, was extremely intoxicated by the time they headed back to the Arizona and Tom ended up carrying him most of the way to the brow. The fight and his argument with Cindy had gotten to him in a pretty big way, and he managed to drink his worries away for the night. The unwritten rule in the Navy is, you must walk up the brow and request permission to come aboard no matter how drunk you are and you had to be professional and polite. If you could manage to do that, you wouldn't be in any trouble for over indulging in alcoholic beverages. Your friends could drag you back to your rack for all anyone cared. Tom and Ralph slapped Jimmy in the face trying to get him coherent enough to make his trip up the brow. When they finally thought he could do it, they forced him to go first, so they could keep an eye on him and prevent him from violating any of the unwritten rules. Although he was somewhat of a sloppy mess, he managed to make it through with the help of Tom and Ralph and even their buddies on watch. Both Tom and Ralph collectively dragged him to his rack so he could sleep it off. It had been a wild night by any normal person's standards. But just another night out on liberty for anyone who has ever sailed with the U.S. Navy. Rough times loomed ahead, and little did anyone know, the isolationist United States was going to be thrust into a war of epic proportions and be a main contributor to complete and total victory.

Hardly anyone could have predicted the historical chain of events that were to happen next.

WINTER 1941

It was December 5th, a relatively quiet Friday afternoon at work turned into a weekend of rest and relaxation for the boys onboard the Arizona and many other ships berthed at Pearl. Training was going to ramp up to the next level in the coming weeks as the United States prepared for what many felt was the inevitable. Although word out of Tokyo was that peace talks were going well and the Japanese and Americans had agreed that no aggressions would be taken upon each other. Even the lowest ranked seaman stuffed in the back of a galley on any ship didn't believe that bullshit. Tensions were high and it was only a matter of time before the powder keg exploded. Nobody was sure when or where, and frankly, the government didn't want to believe it would happen at all. The American people's heart was not into the conflict raging all across the world at the moment. It hadn't hit home for them yet due to the geographical location of the continental United States. Hawaii was the only part of the U.S. close to what may be considered an enemy. In typical fashion, liberty call onboard the Arizona went off without a hitch that Friday night. The sailors, including Jimmy, Ralph, and Tom rolled down the brow into a few days off. The guys had plans that Saturday to finally get Jimmy a car of his own. It was an early 30s Dodge Coupe that was for sale in town. They had seen it in the newspaper. The asking price was $250. That was more than 3 months' pay, but luckily Jimmy had been saving for the past several months due to the fact that they were always underway. Saturday morning they all went with Jimmy when he purchased the car. Right away they took it back to base to the auto hobby shop and got to wrenching. At almost 10 years old, the car needed a little bit of work to be road worthy. Brakes, an oil change and a small tune-up. It was a nice relaxing Saturday. Jimmy was through the roof with excitement at the thought of finally having his own wheels. He couldn't wait to pick up Cindy for dinner that night and surprise her. After a few beers in the garage, they brought the car down off the lift and back outside. It ran like a top and they all were pleased. "Shit, Jimmy this thing runs like a demon!" Tom said. "Might even give my Plymouth a run for her money! We might just have to test that out sometime." He said playfully. "Anytime any place pal!" Jimmy said enthusiastically. They all headed back to the ship to clean up and get ready for their separate nightly festivities. Saturday was always reserved for the girlfriends and some alone time. It was always understood between the three of them that Fridays were for drinking with the boys and Sundays were for relaxing before heading back to work that following Monday. Jimmy strolled down the brow with an extra bit of swagger in his step knowing that he was about to jump into his own car and pick up his lady for a nice romantic dinner and some quality time together. His Dodge strolled towards Cindy's house which happened to be on base. It also happened to be on Admiral's row. Her father was a prominent Two-Star Admiral in the Pacific Fleet. As you can imagine, the first time Jimmy went to her house he was nervous as hell. He had no idea she was the Admiral's daughter! Much to his surprise the Admiral was never there. The few occasions Jimmy did meet him, the Admiral pretended not to know that Jimmy was in the Navy and put on the usual "Be good to my daughter or I'll kill you" act that was enough for Jimmy. They never discussed anything Navy related and Jimmy was thankful the Admiral allowed him to date his daughter. Nothing was different that night. The Admiral wasn't there when Jimmy picked up Cindy, but what was strange was, Cindy told him he hadn't been home in a few days, working excruciatingly long hours. But that wasn't completely out of the norm for a Two Star so Jimmy didn't think anything of it. Cindy was really knocked-out surprised when he rolled up in his new set of wheels. She marveled over the plain Dodge coupe, knowing how important it was to Jimmy. She truly was proud of him and all the hard work and long stints out at sea he had endured to save up the money to buy the car. This made the pride well- up inside of him as they rolled down the street to dinner. Something was in the air that night at dinner but Jimmy just couldn't put his finger on it. It was a relaxing Saturday night and he was glad to be able to spend it with his girl. But something made him uneasy. This was a typical feeling of anyone in any branch of service in those days. It felt as if the powder keg could ignite at any moment and an all-out conflict could be at the doorstep of the United States. Nothing had eluded to the fact in the recent days and things were almost too quiet around the base and even aboard the Arizona. It was as if everyone was in a daze. They finished up their romantic dinner at their favorite little hole in the wall restaurant and jumped back in Jimmy's car. He had plans to take Cindy to the beach that night to look at the stars and the moon. It was a beautifully clear night and he knew she would love the surprise. As they lay on the hood of the Dodge, he turned to Cindy who was basking in the beautiful moonlight with an angelic glow. "There's something I've got to say to you sweetheart." Jimmy said seriously. A nervous look came over Cindy's face as the statement took her by surprise. She didn't say anything but looked intently at Jimmy waiting for what he had to say. "I love you Cindy." Jimmy said shyly not knowing how she'd react. It was the first time either of them had used such a serious word since they had been dating. But he had a lot of time to think about it and he was truly in love with her. She constantly drifted through his mind while he was out to sea and he was always daydreaming about a future with her and little ones running around the yard of their little house with a white picket fence. The

American Dream. Especially for a Japanese Immigrant. He wouldn't tell her any of that right away. He didn't want to overwhelm her. A warmness came over her face almost as if what Jimmy said had been a relief. "I love you too sweetheart. With all of my heart." Cindy said sincerely. The truth of the matter was, they had both been crazy about each other since the first day they met, but were both too stubborn to admit it to each other. Now several months in to dating it finally spilled out. The rest of the night was filled with romance and talking until it was almost early morning and Jimmy had to bring her home. As he rolled up Admirals row to Cindy's house he came to a slow stop. "I had a great time with you tonight. You always know how to light up my life Cindy." He said. "I have an uneasy feeling about what's going on in the world and it might get difficult in the coming weeks. We are going to be underway a lot but I want you to know that I love you and you're always on my mind. I hope you will wait for me because I want a future with you." Jimmy said adamantly. "Of course, I will sweetheart. I just need you to stay safe out there and come home to me. I think we have an amazing future ahead of us. I love you more." Cindy exclaimed lovingly. Jimmy jumped out of the car and opened her door for her. As he walked her to the front door of the house he leaned in for a sweet kiss. They said their goodbyes for now and Jimmy trotted back to the car light as a feather. He was completely in love. Jimmy was on cloud nine as he headed back to the Arizona for some much-needed rest. He couldn't help but take in the absolute beauty of the island at this time of night, soaking in the total moonlight shining down from above. At this point in his life everything was on the right track. Pride streamed through his mind on the ride back to the ship. Pride in his service, pride in his girl, pride in his family, and pride in his status as an American. He knew he would have to call his parents in the morning and tell them the news about Cindy. He couldn't wait for his whole family to meet the girl he loved. Interracial couples were nonexistent back then and he knew that even though he was an American, there would be plenty of hurdles to get over. Many of the people in the U.S. had the same views as Dick Tripton unfortunately, but Jimmy hoped his faithful service in the Navy would earn him respect and allow people to look past his nationality and accept him. Even though he was as American and, in many cases, more American than others, it was a difficult and unfortunate time in our country's history. Jimmy skipped up the brow toward the quarterdeck of the USS Arizona, exchanged formalities with the watch stander, and made his way toward his rack for some shut-eye. Sunday would be a day filled with hanging out with the guys and drinking some beers. Maybe they could even get a game of baseball in with enough people Jimmy thought to himself as he fell fast asleep. Life was good.

DECEMBER 7TH, 1941

A day that will live in infamy...... The clock had just struck 7:55 A.M local time when a thunderous boom awakened Jimmy and just about every other sailor in his berthing. He thought it was strange for any live fire exercises to be happening early on a Sunday morning, not to mention close enough to the island to elicit that loud of an explosion. But these explosions were no exercise. In a split second, the ship abruptly and violently shuddered in the water. The Arizona and the entire rest of the Pacific fleet were under surprise attack by the Japanese. The peace talks in the prior months had been a Trojan Horse, all while the empire of Japan planned to hit the isolationist United Sates in the only formidable force they had at the time. The aging Pacific fleet at Pearl. With every nearby explosion the Arizona rocked back and forth in the water. To this point she had only been strafed and taken a few glancing bomb hits. The scene on board was much like the rest of the island. Absolute chaos. Waves of Japanese fighters dominated the skies above like locusts, all but blocking out the beautiful Hawaiian sunshine over Pearl. They had achieved their goal of absolute surprise. On the Lords day, while sailors rested and worshipped, they delivered a cowardly sucker punch and an undoubtable act of war upon our great nation. As always, our brave men and women rose to the occasion in the best fashion they could. Jimmy, and the other men on board his ship were no different. As he navigated through the chaos on board to try and reach the weather deck and his battle station, he took note of how although it may have seemed like chaos at the time, everyone had a job and a position and they were doing their best to execute their mission. When Jimmy finally reached his battle station and manned up one of the 40mm guns, he began firing at Japanese Zeros overhead. Normally it would take an entire crew of at least three people to operate the turret, but the other members of Jimmy's battle station hadn't made it there yet, so he operated it alone. The Arizona was now engulfed in flames at the bow of the ship and men were working to put out the blaze. Explosions rocked the harbor and fire ravaged many of the ships. So far, the Arizona hadn't faired as bad as the other ships. Jimmy lined his sights up on a zero in the distance that was making a run at the USS Utah. The 40mm gun lurched to life as he spent rounds trying to eradicate the enemy fighter. By this time the rest of his crew had shown up so he was no longer alone and able to make a better attempt at taking down enemy planes. Just as he let up on the trigger, he saw one of his tracer rounds punch a hole right through the rising sun on the side of the zero and it careened toward the water. "How do you like that you son of a bitch!" Jimmy Screamed. In that moment the entire ship seemed to grow legs and lift itself out of the water. In one of the most famous explosions of the war that was caught on film, the forward deck of the Arizona was struck by a 1,760-pound bomb that triggered a massive explosion, lifted the 33,000-ton vessel out of the water and killed 1,177 sailors and Marines instantly. Jimmy's battle station was all the way at the stern of the ship. He was thrown over 100 feet into the water when the blast went off. Barely conscious, Jimmy came to with his head bobbing in and out of the light waves. He had already ingested a lot of seawater and was struggling to breath. He thought in that moment he was going to drown. When suddenly what seemed to be the hand of god, grabbed the back of his collar and lift his head out of the water. It was none other than Dick Tripton who had also somehow survived the infamous blast. He had managed to grab a life vest that had been floating in the water and was in better shape than Jimmy. "I saw you shoot down that bastard Jap Zero before the explosion went off. Forget all that crap I said before. You're one of us, brother." Dick said sincerely while keeping Jimmy's head above water. Eventually they were pulled out by rescuers quite some time later. But not before the Japanese sneak attack decimated the pacific fleet. Thousands of men and women were dead at the hands of the Empire of Japan. Amazingly enough, Jimmy and Dick only suffered minor injuries despite being thrown hundreds of feet when the Arizona exploded. The only thoughts flying through Jimmy's mind after the attacks had ceased were if his friends made it through and more importantly his girl. Cindy was a nursing student and would surely be called to action to help mend injured sailors and civilians. Unfortunately, he would have to wait to learn if his girl and friends were alright. Jimmy had not seen Tom or Ralph since the night before the attack. In the days following, anyone who wasn't badly injured was part of a rescue crew to try and find survivors trapped in ships that had either capsized or sank in the shallow waters of Pearl. It was 5 days after the attack when Jimmy got word, they had found Tom's body in the water near the Arizona. Ralph, like thousands of others was never found. Likely to be inside the Arizona with countless other shipmates who never made it to the surface after she was hit. Cindy was severely injured when a Japanese zero strafed the hospital that she was at. Thankfully through the grace of god she survived the awful ordeal and Jimmy stayed by her bedside as she recovered fully. He couldn't believe that in a split second he had lost his two best friends and came very close to losing the love of his life. If the attack wasn't personal before, it definitely was now. He had a deep fire burning inside him. He would fight this war until the bitter end. To achieve revenge for all his brothers lost. To achieve complete and total victory for the country he loved so dearly. As famously quoted, the Japanese had "Awoken the sleeping giant." And they would soon pay dearly for their actions. The war would be long and bloody. Many Americans and many Japanese would die for their countries in some of the most horrible fighting the likes of which the world had never seen before. Even in the mustard gas filled trenches of the first World War. In his famous declaration of war, the day after the attacks, President Franklin Delano Roosevelt summed up the sentiment throughout the armed forces and the entire country, especially those who had lost loved ones: "No matter how long it may take us to overcome this premeditated invasion, the American people in their righteous might will win through to absolute victory. I believe I interpret the will of the Congress and of the people when I assert that we will not only defend ourselves to the uttermost, but will make very certain that this form of treachery shall never endanger us again. Hostilities exist. There is no blinking at the fact that our people, our territory and our interests are in grave danger. With confidence in our armed forces - with the unbounding determination of our people - we will gain the inevitable triumph - so help us God." At the end of the day, War had been declared, thus beginning a long and arduous road for Jimmy and the rest of the members of the armed forces who would bear this burden of war and see it through to victory.

THE AFTERMATH

In the days following the vicious and deliberate attack on Pearl Harbor, there was a flurry of different emotions sweeping the nation. Weeks and days before the attack, many everyday Americans supported isolationism and preferred not to be involved in what many would call "Europe's War". But the attack on American soil made things very personal. Revenge was in the air and Americans craved it immediately. Nobody since the British had landed an attack on U.S. soil and the Japanese were bound to pay for what they had done. Unfortunately, Japanese Americans were the first to feel the brunt of this anger the American people felt. At a time when racial prejudice was already common place in our country, the current situation in the world only amplified and fanned the flames towards Japanese Americans. Almost all of whom were hard-working, proud contributing members of our society. Most even condemned the attack from their motherland and quickly pledged allegiance to the United States and their fight against the empire of Japan. Unfortunately, that didn't stop President Roosevelt from signing Executive order 9066 on February 19, 1942 effectively creating the internment camps that would affect the lives of over 117,000 Japanese Americans. Many of whom were already citizens. The idea was to prevent espionage activities and thwart a full-scale invasion of the continental United States by Japanese who were already there. While desperate times called for desperate measures and nobody was sure who to trust in those days, it is definitely looked at as a mistake and an extremely dark mark in U.S. History. Many Japanese families were separated from each other and not reunited until after the war, if ever. It was a sunny day in the beginning of March, 1942. Clean up and reconstruction efforts were in full swing at Pearl, and it was an all hands effort. Jimmy had been at it since the days following the attacks. Dick Tripton and Jimmy were miraculously not severely injured in the Arizona explosion. Communication on and off the island was extremely difficult due to the extent of the damage. Jimmy had written letters home to assure his parents that he was okay, but had yet to receive a letter back. News had yet to reach the island of internment camps at the time and he was totally unaware what was happening back on the mainland. It was a Friday afternoon when Jimmy finally received some mail. He was expecting some letters from his family back home expressing their relief that he was alright and had survived the atrocious attacks. What he received instead was a letter from the state department informing him that his father, mother, and sister had been brought to an internment camp in Southern California due to their ties to Japan. Worst of all, they had been separated. His mother and sister were in one camp while they brought his father to a different camp. Jimmy was absolutely heartbroken and furious. How could the country he loved so much and was literally on the verge of dying for just weeks before do this to him and his family? His parents were proud Americans who worked for everything they had and support our nation to the fullest. He was absolutely speechless and lost. But there was nothing he could do but write letters and send them to the addresses enclosed in the state department letter. Hoping and praying that he could reach his family and console them. The entire situation left him lost and wondering "Just exactly how much do I need to do to prove that I belong in this country? That WE belong in this country?" Just then that thought was cut short. The Petty Officer in charge of Jimmy's working party called over to him and said "GM2 Katsumoto! Report to the personnel office immediately. They've got orders for you." "Aye!" Jimmy returned back. "Orders?" he thought to himself. "There are barely any ships left here to man! Where can they possibly be sending me?" As Jimmy strolled smartly into the personnel office, he was immediately handed a folder stamped "Confidential". "GM2 you are to report to the Indy by 1400 hours sharp. They are due to go underway early tomorrow morning with Task Force One. Do not be late!" The chief behind the desk barked. "Aye Chief!" Jimmy spouted back in return as he about faced and walked out of the office. It was like the first day of school all over again for

Jimmy. The only boat he had known in his time in the Navy was the Arizona. Now he would be going to a new one where he didn't know anyone and nobody knew him. At that same moment Dick Tripton was walking into the office as Jimmy was heading out. "Hey Dick, I'm heading to the Indianapolis!" Jimmy said with a bit of excitement. "Holy shit!" Dick said "I hope they give me something good too." As he lurched into the office a bit hesitant. Moments later he burst out through the door with his orders in hand jumping around. "Hey buddy you won't believe it! I'm going to the Indy too!" Dick yelled. Jimmy was relieved in that moment because he would have a friend in a new environment. It's amazing that just a few short months before, he wanted to knock Dick's head off for being a racist bastard. It just goes to show you that people can change and their ideals can also be changed. All in all, Jimmy was just glad to have somebody who had his back and could vouch for him. Being Japanese and in the U.S. Navy was never going to be harder than it was at the current time. But he would do what he knew how to do best. Work hard and keep his nose clean. New adventures were ahead for Jimmy and Dick onboard the USS Indianapolis. It was 1100 so Jimmy had some time before he had to report to the ship. He was so excited he drove up to tell Cindy the news. She was back working in the hospital after she recovered from her injuries helping to mend the thousands of sailors still healing from the attacks. She was just about the bravest person Jimmy knew and he was so damned proud of her. It inspired him to be a better man himself and he knew one day he would make her his wife. In the meantime, he had to break the news to her that he would be going underway again the following day. Although he was excited about the new assignment, he knew that Cindy would be weary. The first reports off the Arizona on the day of the attack was that no one had survived. So, although she had been injured herself, she was coherent enough to hear that news and feared that Jimmy had been killed along with his shipmates. It wasn't until later the next day when Jimmy was able to find Cindy and reunite with her. Ever since then, they had been inseparable. But she knew he had a duty to do and respected that fact. Jimmy had decided from the start that he wasn't going to tell her about his family being put in the internment camps. He knew that would absolutely floor her and he didn't want her to get her Father involved and put him in an awkward position. He would leave that personal battle burning inside him for the months to come. There was nothing he could do for his family right now and there was a war that needed to be fought. The sooner the U.S. achieved total victory over its enemies, the sooner his family would be reunited. Or at least that's how he rationalized it in his head. As Jimmy waited in the lobby of the hospital for Cindy to come out, his mind raced. How would she take the news? Would she be upset? He tried his best to hide his excitement about the assignment when he finally saw her. “Sweetheart, I have some news to tell you.” Jimmy said carefully. “What is it Jimmy?” Cindy said curiously. “Well I received some new orders today to the USS Indianapolis. It’s a heavy cruiser here in Pearl.” Cindy seemed hesitant in the moment but knew that Jimmy loved being out to sea doing what he could for his country. “That’s great honey! I know you’ve been dying to get back out there and join the fight. Although I’ll be extremely worried when you do finally make it back out to sea.” Cindy said with a bit of nervousness in her voice. “That’s the thing, we head out tomorrow morning for an undisclosed amount of time with Task Force One.” Jimmy bluntly broke the news. He could see the worry wash over her eyes in an instant but she quickly hid it away. “Sailors belong out to sea, right? That’s what my father always says.” Cindy stated as a matter of fact. “I’m going to miss you dearly Jimmy but I know you have a duty to do. The hospital will keep me busy while you’re gone and I will write you every day.” She said sweetly. “Of course, sweetheart. I know you have to get back to work but hopefully after I report this afternoon, I will get some liberty tonight. Can I take you out to dinner later?” Jimmy asked. “Pick me up at 6 sailor.” Cindy said with a wink and she was off back behind the double doors to aid more of Jimmy’s fellow brothers. He was in awe of just how strong she was. Even how well she took the news in stride. The truth is, she was used to the Navy life and had to watch her father leave the entire time growing up. If anyone was trained to be with a sailor is was Cindy. Jimmy just hoped one day he could be around long enough to marry her. He hoped this god damned war was over quick. But it would be a long and arduous battle for our country and the rest of the Allies. One that was only just beginning.

UNDERWAY AGAIN

For Jimmy and Dick, being underway again was exactly what the doctor had ordered. After the atrocities they had witnessed during the attack on Pearl, the loss of many friends and shipmates, it was almost therapeutic to be back out to sea again amongst the waves. Life of a sailor out to sea is extremely hectic and busy during peacetime. But we as a country were no longer at peace. We were at war with the empire of Japan. The orchestrator of the single most deadly attack on U.S. soil in over a century. The business kept Jimmy and Dick's minds occupied as they, along with many others, mourned the loss of their friends and family. A sense of revenge floated about the Indy. These boys wanted payback. They wanted a piece of the Japanese badly and couldn't wait to get in the fight. Operations onboard the Indy were fast paced and serious, as the main reason for the underway was to try and locate the Japanese carrier force that had launched the attack on Pearl. Day in and day out the sailors stood watch as task force 12 tried to locate the Japanese. Nobody wanted to seek revenge more than Jimmy having lost his two best friends to the heinous attack. The general feeling aboard the ship was that they were close. So close they could almost taste it. Unfortunately, the fire burning inside all of them would have to wait another day as they were unsuccessful in finding the Japanese. The remainder of the underway was overall uneventful, as they completed training exercises to prepare for the upcoming pacific campaign that they would undoubtedly be a part of. It took some time for Jimmy to get acclimated to the new ship. Things for a Gunner's Mate onboard a cruiser were slightly different than a battleship. The armament was different therefore learning maintenance and firing exercises was also different. After a couple weeks out to sea, Jimmy made the transition quite well and his ability was noticed by his upper chain of command. Although things involving his job were going well, he faced similar backlash from members of the crew for being Japanese. It was nothing that he wasn't already used to. He knew he would have to prove himself and be in the thick of things to earn their respect. He couldn't believe that after going through what he did during the attack, he still had to put up with bullshit racism. But he kept his mouth shut and his head down as was customary of the times. He knew he was going to have to be that much better than the next guy and have everyone's back even though they might not necessarily have his. The truth of the matter was, Jimmy was no less American than any other sailor onboard that ship. He was knee deep in all the blood and guts of the attack on Pearl Harbor. In an odd sort of way, that's what made Jimmy love America so much. It had given him the opportunity to be there and fight for what he loved and the freedoms he held so dear. Even though not everyone may have been happy with his presence. Things were going to change for Jimmy throughout the war. He was a leader and a red-blooded patriot who would easily lay his life down for the guy next to him. No matter what that guy had to say about Jimmy. As the Indy steamed for port, Jimmy knew it was going to be a quick stop before they head out to the pacific campaign. He rehearsed how he would say goodbye to Cindy, not knowing if he would make it home to see her again. As he lay in his rack at night, he tried to write down the things he would say to her. By the end, he had a scratch piece of paper with more scribbles and eraser marks than anything productive. He knew what he was going to say to her had to come from the heart. Hopefully it would come out smooth and ease her of some of the worry. The last thing Jimmy wanted was for Cindy to see that he was frightened about the future. Every soldier and sailor was frightened before heading into battle. The fear is what kept you alive in such difficult and crazy situations. It wasn't necessarily the fear of dying for their country, but the will to want to survive for it and continue the fight. Everyone was down for the cause and although he harbored some fear, Jimmy was ready to dig in and do his part. It was an early Sunday morning when the Indy pulled back into Pearl for supplies and a refuel before heading back out the following morning. Every one of her crew members knew that this Sunday would be their last on solid ground for quite some time. There was work to do in the pacific, and the Indianapolis was going to be right in the middle of it. As everyone who wasn't unlucky enough to draw duty on that Sunday, trotted down the brow, there was an eerie silence. It was a silence of men ready to go to work. Jimmy couldn't help but well up with pride for what he was involved in. He had a relaxing Sunday planned for Cindy that involved grabbing breakfast and heading to the same beach they went to when he first asked her out months before. Things were so different without Ralph and Tom around. They were always the life of the party whenever they all went out. Jimmy's heart filled with anger and sadness for the loss of his dear friends. Cindy could sense that Jimmy was feeling down. "What's the matter sweetheart?" She asked. He couldn't quite get the words together. He wasn't much for talking about his feelings and just reassured her that everything was fine. He didn't need her worrying even further about where his head was at. He still had to break the news to her that he was going to be gone for an undisclosed amount of time. Jimmy looked down towards the sand as he began to tell her about the upcoming deployment when she cut him off. "I know you're going to be gone for a while. I know you are strong and you are going to make it back to me. I will be thinking about you every minute of the day until you do." Cindy blurted out. Jimmy was awestruck and all he could do is grab her and hold her as the both gazed at the beautiful Hawaiian sunset. They and many other couples, were enjoying their last night together. The unfortunate truth was, many of them would not be returning home to their loved ones. Many wives would become widows and many children would have to grow up without Fathers. The reality of War was heartbreaking and difficult for everyone. But the men bucked up and did what they had to do to protect their country abroad. Everyone who remained at home stepped up as well. From the shipyards to the aircraft factories, Americans went to work to support their boys overseas. It was a collaborative effort and couldn't have been done without the immense industry and support system in the states. Japan was about to find out that they truly did awake the "sleeping giant".

BACK IN THE FIGHT

It had been months since the travesty at Pearl Harbor. The U.S. was knee deep in the mud of a World at War. Something they had tried to avoid through years of isolationism. But the fact of the matter was, the rest of the world needed the cowboys and warriors from the United States to help defeat the evil that was the Axis Powers. Americans in battle are an absolute sight to behold. You can throw whatever you have at them and you may as well be kicking a hornet's nest while you're covered in honey. Retreat is not a regular word in the average U.S. soldier or sailor's vocabulary. They are taught from conception as a warrior to push on and push forward, no matter how daunting the task. That held true for the crew of the Indianapolis, who later in the war would be at the forefront of inevitable Victory for the Allies. But for now, they were just getting ready to get their feet wet in combat in the Pacific. The first order of business for Jimmy and the rest of the crew of the Indy came during the New Guinea campaign. She steamed to the South Pacific 350 mi south of Rabaul, New Britain, escorting the aircraft carrier Lexington. Late in the afternoon of 20 February 1942, the American ships were attacked by 18 Japanese aircraft. This was the first bit of combat Jimmy and Dick had been in since Pearl. For a split second during the attack, Jimmy flashed back to that fateful morning in December. He thought about Ralph and Tom for a moment but then his instincts kicked in. He was already at his battle station manning one of the 40mm bofor Anti-aircraft guns. It takes a couple crew to run one of these turrets. Jimmy was the one manning up the weapon and firing at the attacking aircraft. Aerial bombardments happen fast and you need to see the target long before it sees you if you want any chance of shooting one down. As Jimmy sparingly rattled off the 40mm ammunition that was respectively about the size of a soda bottle, he honed in on a Japanese zero that was heading towards the Indy. He led the target to account for the velocity of the aircraft coming towards him and followed the tracer rounds that came out every 10th round. These rounds allowed the gunner to correct their aim and hit moving targets. As the Zero closed in on the ship, Jimmy opened up the bofor and scored several direct hits on the aircraft. This resulted in a trail of smoke and flames that engulfed the cockpit. Jimmy knew he had gotten his target as the Zero floundered into a steep dive and smashed into the waves about 300 yards from the ship. Another confirmed kill for his resume. It felt great finally exacting a bit of revenge for his fallen brothers but he couldn't revel in it too long. The next target came quickly. By the end of the engagement Jimmy had gotten 2 zeros which he was extremely proud of. It really showed to his new crewmates that he was the real deal and hated the Japs just as much as they did. Regardless of his heritage, Jimmy was American. A fact that he would undoubtedly prove throughout the duration of the war. It was all in a day's work for a Gunner's Mate. The task force had kicked ass during this engagement. Of the 18 aircraft, 16 were shot down by aircraft from carrier USS Lexington, while the other two were taken down by Anti-aircraft fire courtesy of Jimmy. The Americans had an extremely formidable fighting force all throughout the theater. The terrifying part for the Japanese was, they were just getting started. Once the industrial war effort picked up speed and was running at 100%, creating ships in weeks instead of months and years, it would be almost impossible for them to keep up. Not to mention that the Allies were willing to stand toe to toe with Japan on any given day of the week. The war would be long and bloody and the Japanese will to fight wouldn't cease to exist until the last day of the war. But they had made a grave mistake dragging us into the fray. The remaining hours of the day after the attack were spent cleaning weapons and cleaning up brass. It was imperative that all the weapons were kept clean and well maintained. You never knew when the next attack would be. Sometimes there wasn't even a chance to clean the weapons before the next wave of attacks. Other times they spent 24 hours manning their battle stations with little to no action. Often times they'd spend the night on deck next to their guns curled up and sleeping. Waiting for the faint sound of Japanese zeros incoming. There was very little off time in the Pacific campaign and time went by quickly for the sailors on board. Before they knew it, the blistering summer months in the Pacific were upon them. A heat that can only be understood by the men who served there. There was no shortage of sun that summer. But the boys stayed busy. Routine operations continued in the Pacific theater as the spring months rolled into deep summer. It was relatively uneventful, but the ship and crew were functioning as a well-oiled machine. Just itching for the next bit of action against the Japanese. In Early August they would get their wish. Indianapolis headed for the North Pacific to support American units in the Battle of the Aleutian Islands. On 7 August, Indianapolis and the task force attacked Kiska Island, a Japanese staging area. Although fog hindered observation, Indianapolis and other ships fired their main guns into the bay. Floatplanes from the cruisers reported Japanese ships sunk in the harbor and damage to shore installations. After 15 minutes, Japanese shore batteries returned fire before being destroyed by the ships' main guns. Japanese submarines approaching the force were depth-charged by American destroyers and Japanese seaplanes made an ineffective bombing attack. In spite of a lack of information on the Japanese forces, the operation was considered a success. The After-action report of the Battle of the Aleutian Islands favored the allies and the men of the Indy had performed well. She was left unscathed and the men that much more battle-hardened warriors.

HOMESICK

The battles at sea were thrilling and Jimmy felt a sense of pride every time he manned his battle station. He was proud to be a part of the crew of the Indy and hadn't felt exile for being of Japanese descent since his first underway. He had proven himself and thing were going well. But like any sailor who has ever been out to sea, loneliness and homesickness consumed him when they weren't busy. Luckily that wasn't often. But even still the nights on watch were lonely and he couldn't help but think of his family who were likely still locked up in internment camps. He wrote to them daily but hadn't received a single piece of mail back. He was unsure of their condition and wellness which ate away at him regularly. He harbored natural resentment for the government for doing this to the ones he loved while he was out in the Pacific supporting the war effort. He tried his best to put it at the back of his mind because he knew he had a job and a duty to do. Part of him hoped if he stood out enough, he'd be able to get his family out of the camps and sent back home to San Francisco where he would move after the war. So, every day he kept pushing forward with his head down doing the only thing he knew how to do, work hard. He also of course, yearned for Cindy on those lonely nights, wondering what she was doing and wondering if she'd wait for him to be back. He kept a picture of her tucked inside one of the pockets of his uniform and would routinely take it out just to catch a glimpse of her smile. It got him through some tough times. What most people don't understand, is that when you are underway on a Navy ship, it gives you some of the most opportune times to think deeply. There are no city lights at night just you and the stars. No loud noises or automobiles just you and the sound of the waves. You really can find out who you are and what's important to you while you are out to sea if you chose to enter that portion of your mind. It can be therapeutic but it can also create anxiety. So, like anything, it should be done in moderation. One of the things that was the hardest during this time for Jimmy was not having Tom and Ralph by his side. They had been together since day one on the Arizona and he missed them dearly. He had made some good new buddies on the Indy and also had become close with Dick Tripton which helped things. But he had a hard time getting over the loss of his two best friends. Unfortunately, he had no time to mourn their loss as he was right back out to sea after the attack. Like many throughout the war, Jimmy had to put the pain deep down inside him and save it for a rainy day. It was something that would eat away at him for the remainder of his days. The scars of war aren't always visible and some men hide it better than others. The fact of the matter is, Jimmy wasn't the only one feeling this way. You could ask every member of the crew if they felt the same way at some point and they would tell you yes. But what made these men special was their ability to push through and stay in the fight. Men like them were the norm across all theaters during the war. They trudged through adversity to triumph over the evil that was the Axis Powers for the good of all human kind. The atrocities being performed by the Japanese and Germans were despicable and would not be tolerated by civilized men. It had to stop, and stop it would. Unfortunately, only after the bloodiest war in history. As night turned into day and Jimmy's watch came to a close, he headed to his rack for some much-needed rest. All of these thoughts still clouded his mind but he was so exhausted he fell asleep just as soon as he hit the pillow. The fight would continue on another day.

THE HEART OF WAR

The Indy and her crew continued to play a pivotal role in the Pacific campaign throughout the middle years of the war. For 1943 and the majority of 1944 the Indy remained in the thick of the action. Providing imperative support on countless different missions during the Allied island-hopping campaign on their way to mainland Japan. Allied commanders knew that the fight would have to be brought to the homeland. Much to the dismay of the troops. They had encountered some of the fiercest fighting from their adversaries throughout the campaign that had ever been seen in the history of the country. The Japanese were warriors and the Samurai way prevented them from surrendering. They would always choose death before dishonor. The fight was far from over for the Allies. Not only were they waging war across the Pacific, they were trying to contain Hitler from taking over all of Europe. It was a classic battle of good v. evil from the very start of the war. The dynamics of that were exposed further as the war raged on. The Axis treatment of POW's (Prisoners of War) was horrific and completely ignored the Geneva Convention. The horror stories told after the wars end told tales of complete lack of human decency especially from the Japanese, who were exceptionally ruthless toward their prisoners. Most men on Navy ships knew that if they were sunk by a Japanese submarine, and survived, they had high chances of being captured. The very thought of that was feared more than the actual sinking of their ship. Lucky for Jimmy and the crew of the Indy, she felt invincible. At least for the time being. As the days turned into months the war dragged on. The Allies had made significant progress in their island-hopping campaign and the U.S. fleet had done astonishingly well against what was supposed to be a superior Japanese Navy. But the industry back in the states was booming and the war material production was through the roof. Ship yards were turning out troop transport ships in 30 days. They were building carriers and battleships in months as opposed to years. It was an industrial effort that had never been seen in the world before. All the major Auto manufacturing companies had converted to war materials. Whether it be tanks, airplanes, boat motors or hull pieces for ships. The effort was just as important as those men fighting on the front lines. Brave women showed up at these factories on a daily basis filling in for the men who were overseas and proving that they were every bit as capable of being welders and ship fitters as any man in the country. Without them, the war effort would have failed. Without each family rationing precious materials such as metals and foods, the men on the front line would've been without the precious ammunition they so desperately needed and most likely would've starved to death. Both the effort at home and on the front lines raged on for 1943 and 1944. Time seemed to pass by slowly but at the same time quickly for Jimmy. He missed Cindy every second of every day. He thought about his parents every day. He still hadn't heard from them or found out any information about their condition which slowly ate away at him. But he remained silent. The last thing he wanted to do was become a distraction onboard, especially in the heart of the fighting and with the crew functioning so well. He finally felt accepted by his shipmates. He felt they saw him as a red blooded American. Just the same as any of them. Willing to die at a moment's notice for any of them or for his country. As early 1945 rolled around the war seemed to be in high gear. On 24 March, Indianapolis spent 7 days pouring 8-inch shells into the beach defenses. During this time, enemy aircraft repeatedly attacked the American ships. Indianapolis shot down six planes and damaged two others. On 31 March, the day before the Tenth Army (combined U.S. Army and U.S. Marine Corps) started its assault landings, the Indianapolis lookouts spotted a Japanese Nakajima Ki-43 "Oscar" fighter as it emerged from the morning twilight and dove vertically towards the bridge. The ship's 20 mm guns opened fire, but within 15 seconds the plane was over the ship. Tracers converged on it, causing it to swerve, but the pilot managed to release his bomb from a height of 25 ft (7.6 m), then crashing his plane into the sea near the port stern. The bomb plummeted through the deck, into the crew's mess hall, down through the berthing compartment, and through the fuel tanks before crashing through the keel and exploding in the water underneath. The concussion blew two gaping holes in the keel which flooded nearby compartments, killing nine crewmen. Jimmy had been on deck during the attack at his battle station doing his best to knock the Jap plane out of the sky. He had been extremely lucky to be on the opposite end of the ship from where the bomb went through the deck. Fortunately enough, he would've been in the mess hall had he been following his typical schedule on board. But when the Battle Station alarm sounded, he had to move quickly. Luckily for Indy, the ship's bulkheads prevented any progressive flooding after the explosion underneath. Indianapolis, settling slightly by the stern and listing to port, steamed to a salvage ship for emergency repairs. Here, inspection revealed that her propeller shafts were damaged, her fuel tanks ruptured, and her water-distilling equipment ruined. But Indianapolis commenced the long trip across the Pacific, under her own power, to the Mare Island Navy Yard. Unfortunately for the Indy, she was now due for extensive repairs and a refit. Jimmy had asked to be reassigned to Pearl during the re-fitting process and repairs. Mostly so he could spend time with Cindy who he had planned to propose to the second the time was right. But also, so he could jump onto another ship if they needed men to head back into the fight. He didn't want to spend time in California in the shipyard while his brothers were out there dying on the high seas and on the front lines. But his request was promptly denied by his superiors much to his dismay. They needed all the men they could get to help assist with the hasty repair process. Rumors were swirling around that something big was on tap for the Indy and her crew but nobody knew anything about it. They were all told to keep their mouths shut and be ready to head back out on short notice when she was back operational. Part of these rumors made Jimmy excited for the future and what he may be a part of. But it also made him nervous. He was going to propose to Cindy. He wanted nothing more than to be with her and start a family as soon as this god forsaken war was over. It made it all the more important to him to make it back to her in one piece. Just then he thought to himself "I haven't seen Cindy in almost 3 years. What if she doesn't love me anymore? I'm going to propose?" Obviously, they had written letters back and forth just about every day during that period but it still made Jimmy uneasy. What if she found someone else or she can't bear the fact that he will be going back out to sea? She may even say no when he proposes. A whole different type of nervousness and anxiety rushed over him as he laid in his rack. Feelings he hadn't even had time to feel while being in theater. All he could do was pray that Cindy kept her promise to him before he left. The next several months in California would seem like an eternity for Jimmy. But he had made it this long without seeing his lady. He knew he could hang in there for a few more months. In the end, finally seeing her smile would make it all worth it.

A LOVE NEVER LOST

With the Indianapolis finally pulling into Pearl after months of being in California, Jimmy could hardly contain his nervousness and excitement to see Cindy. He hoped that she would be on the pier to jump into his arms. But he was not able to tell her through letters when they would be pulling back in due to security reasons. He had hoped she heard through rumors at the hospital that the Indy was due in that picturesque Friday morning. The Hawaiian sun danced off the water as the ship glided to a rest at the pier. As customary, everyone was in their whites looking crisp and sharp. Walking with the swagger that you only obtain after you've been in combat at sea. The men were battle hardened now and you could see the fatigue on their freshly shaved faces. But they were eager to get back in the fight and end this miserable war once and for all. As Jimmy rounded the corner after climbing down the brow, he immediately spotted that familiar sweet smile that always seemed to melt away his worries. Cindy was wearing a floral sundress and had clearly spent quite some time that morning getting ready to see Jimmy. Jimmy was so happy he could barely get any words out when he embraced her in his arms. "I've missed you so much." He barely stuttered out. He just held her and didn't want to let go. He could have stood there all day. The world around them was frozen in time. The love of his life was finally back in his arms after almost 3 years and he couldn't be happier. In that moment their future flashed before his eyes and he couldn't wait to ask her to be his wife. But that would come later. He had something extremely special planned for that and he just prayed she would say yes. She was everything he ever wanted in a woman. Jimmy had a few days of liberty before he had to report back to the Indy to get underway again. Their next trip was shrouded in mystery. Nobody seemed to know where they were heading or why. He tucked his curiousness into the back of his mind. Right now, he had more important things to worry about. He had to plan the most perfect evening that would lead into him asking the woman of his dreams the most important question of their lives. His plan was rather simple but extremely thoughtful and romantic. He planned to take Cindy to the exact restaurant they met at "The Shack" for dinner. He had already contacted the owner and had a special secluded table set up for the two of them with a view of the ocean. After dinner they would jump into his 30' Dodge and head to the secret beach spot they all had went to the very first day they met. The one that had the beautiful cliffside view. His plan was to make it there just before the sun began to set. With the most breathtaking sunset as their back drop, Jimmy would drop down on one knee and ask Cindy to be his wife. He could barely contain the butterflies in his stomach. Just the thought of the beautiful sunset glowing in her eyes as he proposed was the driving force to make sure everything went perfectly. Cindy could tell that he was up to something because she knew him well. But she had no idea what he had in store for her that evening. It would be one of the best days of her life. As they jumped into Jimmy's coupe and headed toward "The Shack" for dinner they caught up. Although it's almost impossible to even scratch the surface in a 15-minute car ride when you haven't seen each other for two years. Jimmy had tons of sea stories to tell her and tales of the few ports they pulled into, but he was absolutely enamored listening to Cindy tell him about life at the hospital and the rebuilding effort that had been going on at Pearl since the attack. Cindy represented the impeccable strength our nation showed during the war and the immense resilience needed to continue the war effort and for good to defeat evil. He was so proud that they both could be a part of what would undoubtedly go down in American History as either the greatest victory or the most crushing defeat. It was up to the strong will of the American people to ensure victory and they were certainly on the correct path. They sat down for dinner at the special secluded table outside that Jimmy had arranged. "How did you manage to set this up? You just got off the ship hours ago!" Cindy said impressed. "I'd go to the ends of the earth to show my lady a romantic evening."

Jimmy said smoothly. As they both relished in each other's company while watching the daily beach-goers prepare for the sunset, Jimmy couldn't help but daydream about what their life was going to be like together. In a perfect world the U.S. would win the war and he would be able to come home and start a family in a nice little house with a white picket fence. Then the gut-wrenching feeling hit him like a ton of bricks. His family was still interned in camps and he had little idea of their well-being. He felt extremely guilty that in all the excitement of the day he has let that thought slip his mind if only for a moment. He knew that before he could begin living his version of the American dream, he would have to see his Parents freed from their wrongful imprisonment and start the healing process toward forgiving the nation he loved so much for wronging his beloved family. This was the main driving force in why Jimmy fought so hard. He felt that maybe the faster they defeated the Japanese and witnessed how hard he fought against them, it would in turn, materialize into the release of his family and so many other Japanese- Americans who had been interned at the beginning of the war. But he knew there was nothing he could do until they won the war. So that's what had to be done. As fate would have it, the moment after their dinner was brought out to the table, Jimmy noticed one of the Chiefs from the Indy all but burst into the restaurant looking around feverishly. He had a bad feeling. Finally, they made eye contact and the chief made his way over to their table. He politely introduced himself to Cindy and asked Jimmy if they could have a word in Private. "GM2, an immediate recall has been issued and we all need to report back to the Indy within the next 45 minutes. I'm sorry but its urgent. We are set to get underway before the stroke of midnight." Jimmy was absolutely crushed. This ruined his entire plan of asking Cindy to marry him. The Chief could see the distress in Jimmy's expression. "Listen son, finish up dinner with your lady and if I were you, I'd hang onto that beauty for a long time." The chief smiled. "I'll stall your muster as long as I can but you need to be back to the ship within the hour." "Thanks, Chief." Jimmy replied respectfully. He knew he had a direct order and there wasn't much he could do about it. But he would be damned if he wasn't going to make Cindy his Wife that night one way or another. It may be a lot less romantic than he had hoped but, either way, it would happen. As he made his way back to the table Cindy could tell something was seriously wrong. "You're going back out, aren't you?" she asked feverishly. "Yes. We are pulling out tonight. I need to be back on the ship within the hour." Jimmy said solemnly. Cindy was even more crushed than Jimmy but she tried to hide it. She knew how hard it was on him and didn't want to make it worse. Instead, she encouraged him and told him that time would fly by. Just as the previous 2 years had. In that moment, she was the bright light on one of his darkest days. He immediately dropped down on one knee and presented her with a simple wedding band he had managed to pick out during his travels. She was in absolute shock. "I had a much more romantic plan for our evening." Jimmy said slightly disappointed. "But Uncle Sam seems to have decided otherwise. But I will be damned if I go back out on that god forsaken boat without you back here waiting to be my wife." Jimmy exclaimed. "And when I do come back, this war will be won and I will be home for good that's a promise." Jimmy said confidently. Cindy could barely contain herself as she let out a little squeal "Yes! Of course, I'll marry you! It's all I've wanted since you have been away!" She said with her eyes welling up with tears. "You just make sure you make it home safe to me do you understand? Whatever you have to do you must make it back to me." She implored. All Jimmy could do in that moment was embrace her and give her the biggest hug and kiss he could muster up. It was a moment filled with joy and hope for the future. But also, a moment filled with doubt and uncertainty about his next mission. His emotions were stronger than the roughest seas he had encountered. But he knew he had all the reason in the world to make it home safe and he would stop at nothing to do so. The next few months may be uncertain, but one thing was for sure, he loved Cindy with all of his heart.

THE BOMB

The Indianapolis did indeed pull out that night like the Chief had told Jimmy. He just made it back to the ship in time before he was late for muster (Role call). There was a buzz about the ship. Nobody knew what their next mission was but the rumors spread about the ship like wildfire. It was obviously something top-secret because the higher ups had tight lips about their destination. All the sailors knew was they were on their way back to the Pacific theater, but this time they were to deliver something of immense importance to the war effort. While in California, Jimmy had noticed a higher level of brass aboard the Indy while they were in the yards. This wasn't extremely unusual as many of the admirals liked to personally check up on the progress of a ship and when they were slated to be able to rejoin the war effort. So, he hadn't thought much about it. Apparently, the Indy was carrying extremely precious cargo which may be why only engineering sailors were allowed lower than the mess deck spaces. Eventually rumor got around that they were carrying some components of a new bomb that was more powerful than anything the world had seen. Their destination was Tinian. It was amazing what the Enlisted underground could find out by over hearing conversations the brass were having. All of the sailors aboard the Indy were beaming for the 6-day trip that was rather fast but uneventful. They all felt that they were part of something special. Hopefully something that would put an end to this god forsaken war and send them all home. That was something that was weighing especially heavy on Jimmy's mind, given he had just proposed to Cindy before they left in a hurry. He absolutely couldn't wait to be back home and get started on his American Dream with a house and a family and even a little white picket fence. Most importantly getting his family reunited and out of those terrible internment camps where they had spent most of the war. He knew the Indy had to take care of business before any of that could happen though so he tried his best to stay focused on the task at hand. The Gunner's Mates were assigned the security watches to monitor the package while aboard the ship. Anything ordnance related was their responsibility. So once a day, Jimmy stood guard in front of precious cargo of unknown contents. They were briefed before they stood the watches not to touch or let the packages out of their sight as well as to shoot anyone who disregarded the rules. This seemed excessive to Jimmy but he was determined to follow all orders given to him if it meant protecting national security. Luckily, nobody got nosey enough to test these orders. They left Pearl on the 19th of July 1945 and ended up at the Island of Tinian on the 26th of July. An almost record setting pace at almost 33 miles per hour. The seven-day trip was rather uneventful but excitement was definitely spreading like wildfire throughout the ship and the mess decks. Tales of the U.S. defeating Japan in a sort of comic book style victory were woven by young sailors of all different types of backgrounds. They all had one thing in common. They loved their country enough to die for it. When the Indy finally pulled into port to deliver her sensitive cargo, the boys were ready for a bit of liberty. After offload, the captain authorized a few hours of liberty before they were to report back to the ship that night. Underway was set for early the next morning because the she was due in Guam by the 28th of July. Jimmy and Dick Tripton had shot the shit during the leg from Pearl to Tinian and had decided to go grab a few beers if they were afforded the time. As they walked across the bow and departed the ship, both of them knew as self-respecting Navy men, that a few beers would most certainly turn into a few cases of beer. Before they knew it, it was 2230 and they were due to report back to the ship by the top of the hour. Jimmy, Dick, and several dozen other sailors from the Indy had drank the local bar completely dry in a matter of hours. It was rare during the war for them to get any kind of liberty overseas due to the extremely operational tempo of the Pacific campaign. When they pulled in for fuel and supplies, they were typically only in port for a few hours while stores were packed aboard the ship and she was refueled. The rest of the replenishments were done at sea. So, Jimmy and the boys definitely got their money's worth in Tinian. Little did they know they had just been a part of history. Delivering the components of what would be the world's first Atomic bomb, designed to bring the empire of Japan to their knees in the coming months. As Jimmy and Dick did their best to drunkenly stumble back to the ship and climb into their racks, they passed the skipper of the boat who looked at them with a little bit of disgust but at the same time, knew his sailors worked their tails off for him. "Go on and get to bed sailors. You better not be late for duty in the morning and better have a fresh shave!" The skipper said half-heartedly but still stern enough for Jimmy and Dick to snap to a half drunken attention and reply "Yes Sir!" while they continued to stumble down to the berthing. The life of a sailor underway was always interesting. You never knew what would happen next. The entire crew of the Indianapolis was about to find out just how true those words would ring in the coming days. But for now, it was time for the men to sleep off the buzz they acquired and prepare for the undoubtable hangover of the next morning.

JULY 30TH, 1945

The clock had just rolled over from 2359 to 0000 signifying the change of day from the 29th to the 30th of July on board the Indy. She was in transit toward Guam where the crew would be receiving training before heading to join Task Force 95 in Okinawa to continue on the fight. Most of her crew, those who weren't on duty or manning their underway posts, were sound asleep in the berthing spaces. There is nothing quite like the stillness in the middle of the night of a warship underway. It's the loudest silence you'll ever hear. But a silence all the same. You can hear the sound of the waves lapping on the side of the hull as she makes way through the water toward her destination. You can hear the sounds of her main powerplant providing the necessary propulsion allowing her to cut through the vast unknown of the open sea. It's an extremely peaceful time for a sailor. While many lie fast asleep, there are many who lie awake thinking. Thinking of when they'll be home next. About what the war has in store for them and their fellow crewmembers. Would they make this hasty journey safe? Or was danger lurking in the depths of the ocean, ready to disrupt the stillness of the night. Jimmy was one of those sailors with a lot weighing on his mind so he lie awake. His watch had just struck 0014 and all remained silent. He knew that if he didn't get some rest, the following day would be long a grueling. He rolled over in his rack and finally closed his eyes in hopes of drifting off into a relaxing sleep. Less than a minute later at 0015 all hell broke loose aboard the USS Indianapolis. Jimmy and the entire crew were violently removed from their racks and sent to the deck by one of the most violent explosions he had felt since being aboard the Arizona during the Pearl Harbor Attack. The General Quarters alarm whaled instructing sailors to man their battle stations but it was too late. Deep in the cover of darkness of the depths of the Pacific Ocean, a Japanese submarine had preyed upon the Indy as she lumbered through the water at 25 knots. The Jap Sub had slammed two type-95 torpedoes into the side of Indy both on her starboard side. One struck the bow and the other amidships. Luckily for Jimmy and the fellow sailors in his berthing space, they were on the opposite side of the ship, away from where the torpedoes struck. Hellfire and brimstone consumed the Indianapolis as secondary fires and explosions ravaged the warship. She took on a heavy list as she began to take on massive amounts of sea water through her wounds. Jimmy had a severe head injury from being thrown from his rack onto the deck. He managed to get an old t-shirt wrapped around his head to stop the bleeding. As he felt the violent list of the ship to the starboard side, he knew from his experience at Pearl that it wouldn't be long before she was capsized and on the bottom. He knew he had to act extremely fast to help who he could make it to the weather deck and abandon ship. Although not necessarily favorable, in order to survive, the crew would be making the plunge into the water in the dead of night. Jimmy rounded up the other sailors in his berthing "Let's fucking go! Everyone to the weather deck!" Jimmy yelled incessantly. Many of the men were stilled dazed from being woken up out of a dead sleep and thrown to the ground. In less than 12 minutes Indy would be capsized and heading toward the bottom. The men had to act fast or they would be taking the unwanted ride to their final resting place. As the navigated the P-ways and ladder wells of the heavily listing ship toward the outside air and the weather deck, Jimmy couldn't help but notice the immense damage caused by the torpedo attack. He was horrified and immediately his mind took him back to the Arizona where he lost his two best friends. He knew he didn't have time to be scared but he also worried for his buddy Dick Tripton who was berthed on the other side of the ship, close to where the torpedoes struck the hull. Jimmy feared the worst but would sort out his emotions after he and the other men were safely off the ship. When they reached the port side of the weather deck, Indy was listing so hard to the starboard side, they all had to hang onto the railing to keep from sliding across the deck to an untimely death. Jimmy ordered the men with him to abandon ship as they all leapt over the side into the dark of night.

Once in the water they all followed the training they had received which taught them to get as far away from the vessel as fast as they could. This was to avoid being sucked under when the massive warship finally sank below the surface. When the men finally got a safe distance away, they turned around and the USS Indianapolis had disappeared below the waves of the Pacific. Another casualty to the World at War. But Jimmy was alive. Somehow through the grace of god he had survived his second ship of the war sinking. Not many of the crew were as fortunate as Jimmy and the men in his berthing. Of the 1,195 crewmembers, some 900 made it into the water. The other were either killed instantly in the attack or became trapped below deck when she capsized and slipped beneath the waves. None of the men in Jimmy's group had life jackets, so all were just treading water at the moment. They began searching for debris to help them stay afloat. They were fortunate enough to come across a non-inflated life raft that was released from the deck of the Indianapolis as she went down. Unfortunately, there was not enough room for all 25 men in the area to fit, so many of them had to hang on the outside with their legs in the water. The men took turns being inside the raft and hanging off the side. While the Japanese submarine stalked the Indianapolis like a predator on prey that night, some 900 survivors of the attack would get a glimpse at another terrifying predator lurking in the depths over the next few days. That predator had a taste for blood and could smell it in the water. It would relentlessly torment the sailors as they waited for rescuers who had no idea they had even gone down. That predator was the ruthless and unforgiving Whitetip and Tiger shark.

THE HIDDEN ENEMY

As daylight broke over the horizon and the warm sun began to fall upon the survivors, many questions arose amongst the men. Would they be rescued? Was a distress signal given after they were hit? When were they even due in Guam? Everything had been so rushed and in secret that many of the men had, for lack of a better word, a sinking feeling about their recue hopes. They remained optimistic the first full day adrift. As the sun kissed the tips of the waves it revealed a large debris field from the Indy. Anything that could float was on the surface including the bodies of many sailors who either didn't make it through the night due to their injuries, or drown trying to make it off the ship. As the day went on, the sun became intense and the heat of the South Pacific almost unbearable for the men. They had a complete lack of food and fresh water to combat against starvation and dehydration. By late afternoon the sun had already taken its toll on the men in Jimmy's group. Sun blisters began to form on the men's lips and neck. Their mouth's so dry they couldn't muster enough saliva to lick an envelope if they wanted to. As the men rotated in and out of the raft to give each other much needed rest, they began noticing disturbances on the surface of the water in the debris field.

By dusk, it became apparent that a lot of the floating bodies had disappeared. They had thought nothing of it, chalking it up to becoming waterlogged and sinking to the bottom until Jimmy saw something that would haunt his memory forever. As he leaned over the side of his raft to switch spots with a sailor named Tim Johnson. He was a second class cook in the galley whom everyone knew because he cooked most of their meals. As Jimmy grabbed Tim's hand to pull him into the raft Tim let out an ear-piercing scream and the water turned crimson red around the raft. Jimmy still had a hold on Tim's hand as he screamed in pain. That's when the men got their first glimpse of the hidden enemy lurking below. The dark lifeless eye of a Tiger shark broke the surface as it gnawed on Tim's legs while the men tried to pull him into the raft. They say a shark's eye are like a doll's eyes. Black. Lifeless. Without a thought in the world other than to eat. Before the men could pull him in, the shark broke the surface and took the rest of Tim's torso below the surface. Blood surrounded the raft as all the other men immediately scattered away. The only problem now was, they were surrounded by blood and that tiger wasn't the only shark in the water. The other men began feeling things brush alongside their legs and bump their thighs as the feeding frenzy began. One by one men let out screams and the water turned crimson. It wasn't just in Jimmy's group either. All of the survivors were being targeted throughout the debris field and the other rafts that managed to be utilized. The men in the rafts were helpless. If they all piled in the rafts, they would sink and all be vulnerable to the sharks. The massacre went on for several days in the open ocean. The men's hopes of being rescued dwindled and dehydration and delirium had set in amongst the survivors. Coupled with the crippling fear of the sharks and the horrific scene of watching their friends being stalked and eaten one by one while they watched helplessly. Jimmy never thought that he'd have to worry about anyone other than the Japanese trying to kill him throughout the war, but they had nothing on the sharks and the harsh sun. He prayed often that he would make it out alive. The thought of Cindy receiving the news that he had been killed in the Pacific pushed him forward to adapt and survive. The men ate small rations of spam and whatever else they salvaged from the debris of the wreck. Freshwater was pretty much nonexistent so the men were becoming weak and losing hope. The days were excruciatingly hot and the night bitterly cold. Most men who were in the water had either succumbed to hypothermia or been taken by the sharks. The only survivors alive remained in the rafts and on floating debris that kept their extremities out of the water and away from the murderous sharks. All hope seemed to be lost among the 300 or so men that managed to survive the onslaught. Until on the morning of August 2nd almost 3 and a half days after the Indianapolis went down, a dull buzz was heard on the horizon. Many of the men were in such rough shape that they didn't even notice or hear the sound of an aircraft approaching. Many attributed it to the delirium of their intense dehydration or possibly their imagination. But Around 10:25 am a PV-1 Ventura spotted the survivors adrift. They immediately dropped a life raft and radio transmitter and notified all surface and air assets available to provide assistance of the adrift men's location and coordinates. The first rescue crew to arrive was aboard a PBY-5A Catalina. An amphibious aircraft. Against orders, the pilot decided to land the plane in 12ft swells. He managed to get 56 survivors on board but the plane was then rendered unflyable. Jimmy managed to make it aboard this aircraft with several other survivors as they spent the night waiting for the rescue ships to arrive. Later the next day several ships were able to rescue the rest of the men who were badly injured and dehydrated. Of the 900 men that went into the water when she sank, only 300 survivors were plucked from the pacific. The rest either drown, succumbed to their injuries from the torpedo attack, or were taken by the sharks. It would go down as the largest shark attack on humans in history. As Jimmy walked the deck of the destroyer that rescued him, he searched among the survivors for Dick Tripton. He feared the absolute worst based on where Dick was sleeping on the ship when it was attacked. As he rounded the corner, he heard an extremely familiar laugh. When he looked up, he saw none other than his buddy Dick! Jimmy ran over in excitement but noticed that Dick was pretty frail. So just short of hugging him he went and shook his hand. "I'm glad you made it buddy. I thought the god damned Japs got another one of my friends." Jimmy said in his sarcastic forced American accent. "I wasn't worried about the damned Japs it was those god damned sharks. I had to fight off more than one just to stay alive." Dick said fiercely. "Good news!" Jimmy Exclaimed. "I heard they are sending us back to the states!" he said a bit excitedly. All the men around seemed to revel in the fact that the war may be over for them. They had sacrificed a tremendous amount to overcome evil. They had been successful in their mission to deliver the components of the weapons that would finally bring Japan to their knees. For several survivors of the Indianapolis sinking, including Jimmy and Dick, this was the second ship they watched find a home at the bottom. Two too many if you ask any of them. But that was the name of the game and all a part of war. They witnessed many enemy ships meet the same fate. All they could hope for was peace in the waning days of the deadliest conflict in history.

VICTORY IN JAPAN

For the surviving crew members of the USS Indianapolis sinking, the war was just about over. After they were plucked from the South Pacific during the rescue, they were immediately sent to Guam to recover from their injuries and regain the strength needed to make the Journey back to Pearl, where they would serve the remaining days of the war. The first thing Jimmy did when he got to Guam was try to get ahold of Cindy. He knew that news of the sinking would travel fast, and with her Father being an Admiral, she would almost certainly be worried sick. The Mission was so secretive that the mainland U.S. didn't hear about it until the survivors had already made it to Guam. Jimmy had a hell of a time trying to get ahold of anyone in Pearl including Cindy. After numerous tries, he did what he had to do. He called up her Father on his personal line. "Sir?" Jimmy said nervously. "It's GM2 Katsumoto, I just wanted to let you know that I survived the sinking of the Indy and I'm in Guam. If it isn't too much to ask, can you inform your daughter? I can't get ahold of her and I'm terrified she's worried sick." Jimmy said. "Of course, Jimmy, I'll let her know. Glad to hear you made it through that hell hole. We will talk when you get back to Pearl. Out." The Admiral said and hung up. Jimmy was one of the lucky survivors. He had no major injuries other than the extreme dehydration and sun poisoning. It would be a week or so before Jimmy would hop on the next ship bound for Pearl Harbor. He spent his days in Guam resting and helping with the other survivors. All he could think about now that the war was coming to an end, was getting home to Cindy and reuniting himself with his family. While Jimmy was recuperating in Guam, on August 6th, 1945 news came out that the United States had used a new type of weapon against Japan in hopes of forcing their surrender before an invasion of the mainland was necessary. This new weapon painted scenes of horror on the Japanese town of Hiroshima. It effectively leveled the entire city in a 40-mile radius from the detonation zone killing and destroying everything in its path. The new weapon was the Atomic Bomb. The same bomb that the Indy had delivered crucial parts for to Tinian just before she was sent to the bottom of the Pacific. The Atomic bomb had undoubtedly changed the course of history and the way warfare would be conducted in the decades to come. News of the devastation caused by the bomb spread like wildfire throughout the ranks of the military and even on the home front. Everyone, including the top brass of the U.S. military all the way down the enlisted ranks to regular guys like Jimmy, was sure that this would in fact, cause Japan to finally unconditionally surrender. President Truman threatened Japan with another atomic weapon. Unfortunately for the civilians of Nagasaki, the Japanese government and military called President Truman's bluff. On August 9th, 1945 the second bomb was dropped and detonated roughly 1,000 feet above the city of Nagasaki. Originally destined for the city of Kokura "Fat Man" as the bomb was named had to be redirected to Nagasaki due to inclement weather. The devastation caused by the bomb was equally as horrific as the bomb dropped on Hiroshima but in the end, a necessary evil. If the United States hadn't forced Japan to surrender, an invasion of mainland Japan would've been mounted and executed. It's undeniable that millions of lives would've been lost on both sides and some of the most brutal fighting would have encompassed such a large-scale invasion. The goal was to bring the Empire of Japan to its knees. "Little Boy" and "Fat Man" did exactly that. Jimmy and the other survivors of the Indy couldn't believe how large of a part they had played in the defeat of Japan. Without that delivery, the first bomb would've never been dropped and who knows what would've happened. The general mood around the men was pure excitement at the thought of the end of the war looming. That day finally arrived on August 15th, 1945 when Emperor Hirohito accepted the terms of the Potsdam Declaration, effectively agreeing to an unconditional surrender. Everyone who was anyone on the island of Guam broke out in celebration and cheers. All around the U.S. people flooded the streets to celebrate the end of the deadliest War in the History of the world. Good had finally triumphed over evil as FDR had promised the days after the Pearl Harbor attack. The world of many wars finally had a sliver of peace. Jimmy was elated, but he knew he had a long journey back home with work to do once he got there to reunite his family not to mention and a beautiful Fiancé waiting for him. Jimmy hopped aboard a troop transport ship headed for Pearl a few days after VJ Day. He could barely contain his excitement over the next several days of his journey. The war had been long and exhausting but he had made it. More importantly he had made a difference for the love of his country and for the love of his fellow countrymen. Jimmy was as much of a patriot as anyone else who had spilled their blood for their country. Nobody would ever be able to take that from him. In the meantime, it was time to go home. Time to heal. The nation was battered badly, but she was victorious. God bless America and the Navy Hymn played on the speakers of the troop transport ship as they glided across the pacific. Men were strewn about the deck playing cards or shooting the shit. It was the first time any sort of relaxation had happened in months. These same troop ships brought many young men to what would be their final resting place. A sobering thought that put a damper on the excitement as many men paid their respects to those lost during the war. Even if it was just with their thoughts.

HOMECOMING

As the packed troop ship lumbered into Pearl, a wave of different emotions rushed over Jimmy. They passed by the wreck of the Arizona, still sleeping in the same spot where she sank on that fateful day. The day Jimmy lost his two best friends and the United Sates was thrust into the war to end all wars. Tears streamed down his face as he thought of Tom and Ralph and the memories they had together. Deep down he felt guilty. Guilty that he had made it and they didn't. Not only did he make it through the sinking of the Arizona, but also the sinking of the Indy. Why had he been so lucky throughout the war? Why did he deserve to live? These questions would likely never be answered but Jimmy knew that the best way he could honor his buddies and the rest of those lost during the war, was to live his life with a purpose and with meaning. He would make a difference in the world no matter how big or small that difference would be. He would be a fantastic husband to Cindy, because those men would never get the chance. He would hopefully get the chance to be a fantastic and loving father to his children because those men gave up that opportunity for their country. He would make certain that he didn't waste a moment of his life that he was so blessed to have. As the ships whistle sounded, signifying the ship was moored, Jimmy began scanning the thousands of people on the pier waiting for their sailor. He tried his hardest to find Cindy but of course it was almost near impossible. He would have to navigate the bands, the confetti, and the crying wives to try to find his own crying fiancé. It was a feeling he had never experienced in his entire life. Being completely immersed in such an extreme amount of joy and relief. He was receiving hugs from complete strangers and for the first time he truly felt that nobody saw his nationality when they looked at him. All they saw was an American hero. He couldn't help but tear up and beam with pride. As he sifted through the crowd, he came around the corner where a beautiful brunette stood with her perfect dimpled smile. Jimmy dropped his sea bag and ran to her. She jumped into his arms and they twirled around kissing and hugging like it was the first and last time they'd ever get a chance to. When Jimmy finally set Cindy down, they kept their hands on each other's faces just reveling in the fact that the war was over and they were finally going to be together forever. "I missed you so much my love." Jimmy could barely get the words out over his pure joy. "I was so worried about you when I heard the news about the Indy. I thought I was never going to see you again." Cindy said fighting through tears of joy. "I told you I was coming back to you, it didn't matter what I had to do. Our future together helped me push through and survive. I love you So much Cindy."

Jimmy said embracing her again. The pier was full of thousands of similar interactions between girlfriends and boyfriends and husbands and wives and children. Some men were meeting their children for the first time and becoming fathers in that very moment. You couldn't fit the amount of joy and excitement on that pier in the largest building on earth. Tears were flowing and hugs and kisses were abound. These brave men had brought victory home with them from the Pacific Theater. Without them, it wouldn't have been possible for good to triumph over evil. The entire U.S. was lit up like a firework and the party wouldn't stop for weeks. Alcohol flowed like water and victory parties raged into the hours of the night. It was over and out of the war, the U.S. came out a superpower. It would set the stage for an economic boom in the years to follow and the decade of the 1950s would be one of the best in our country's history. It wouldn't have been possible without the blood and guts of the young men who gave their everything in the Pacific and European Theater. Not only defeating the unimaginable evil of Hitler and the Germans but also defeating the Evil and ruthlessness of the Empire of Japan. The country had banded together and worked as a machine to produce the most war materials in the history of the world in the shortest amount of time. From the home effort to the frontlines, America showed her true grit and determination. As Jimmy and Cindy finally made it off the pier and out of the celebration, they finally had some alone time to revel in each other's presence for a bit. They laid on the hood of Jimmy's Dodge just watching the sunset. Not speaking much just thankful. Thankful for each other. Thankful for the beautiful future that laid ahead of them. Jimmy couldn't wait to get started building his own version of the American dream. But first he had to be reunited with his family. He immediately began making calls to find out their location. He enlisted the help of Cindy's father, Admiral Jacobsen, to find out that they had been released from an Internment camp in California about a month ago. He was even able to retrieve a number at the apartment complex they were supposed to be living at. His hands trembled as he dialed to phone just hoping to hear a familiar voice on the other end of the line. "Hello" the voice on the line was muffled but recognizable. "Dad!" Jimmy cried out with excitement. "I made it I'm home!" he said. "Jimmy! You have no idea how relieved I am to hear from you, son." His father said with a tired and weary voice. "Dad I'm so sorry for what they put you through. I heard about the camps..... I..." His father cut him off before he could finish. "Don't worry about that Jim it's over with. the war is over and hopefully things will go back to normal." His father said. "I have so many things to tell you about Dad. So much happened. How is everyone else? How is Mom and Sarah?" he asked eagerly. "Mom didn't make it out of the camp Jim. I'm sorry to have to tell you like this." His father said somberly. Jimmy felt the wind taken out of him and an immense wave of sadness for the loss of his mother. "I'm coming home in a couple weeks Pop. I'll be there for you guys. I will see you soon." Jimmy said choking back tears as he hung up the phone. He told Cindy the news and she just held him as he cried. After all he had been through and all the blood he spilt for his country, his mother was taken from him while in one of those God damned camps. "For what? For nothing!" Jimmy screamed out in anger through his tears. Jimmy's Mother wasn't the only one who was lost in the camps and something that will forever be a dark stain on the amazing victory the United States built during World War II. Unfortunately, it was seen as a necessary evil by the U.S. Government. Jimmy and his father never held a grudge against the country for the loss of his mother, although angry they understood the hysteria after the attack on Pearl. Understanding wouldn't bring her back though and they'd have to carry on life without her. But at the very most they all would always have each other.

THE AMERICAN DREAM

After the Treaty was signed and the war finally came to an official close, Jimmy served out his remaining weeks in the Navy in Hawaii where it had all started for him a few years prior. It was the place he made some of the best friends he's ever had. It was the place he met the love of his life and the woman he planned to build a future with as his wife. It was where he survived the atrocious attack that thrust the United States into the Second World War. But most importantly, it's where Jimmy finally felt he had been accepted as an American. After the war was over and word of his exploits got out, nobody looked at him like he was the enemy anymore because he was of Japanese descent. They looked at him as an American hero. Like many of the boys who spilled their blood and guts overseas were. He was part of a fraternity of men who were willing to die for their freedom and the freedom of their countrymen back home. As his time in the Navy came to a close, he reflected upon all the great memories and people he met while he was in. Him and Cindy made arrangements to move to California to be closer to Jimmy's family and begin building their American dream. Cindy's Father, Admiral Jacobsen had received an assignment in California so she would be near him as well. When they finally made it to California, Jimmy was able to scrounge up enough money to set him and Cindy up in a little house with a little plot of land just outside San Diego, about a half an hour drive from where his father and sister were living in the city. His plan was to renovate the little house and make it big enough to move his father and sister in to live with them. After all they had been through during the war, he felt it was his duty to make sure they were protected and taken care of. Later that summer, Jimmy and Cindy finally got their wish and got married on the beach in San Diego with a beautiful sunset as their back drop. It was a small ceremony with just a few family and friends which is exactly how they had dreamt it would be. Jimmy had invited his only remaining best friend from the war Dick Tritpton, but had never heard back from him. He assumed Dick had his own life to build and had a lot going on so he wasn't upset. After they said their vows and officially tied the knot, Jimmy scanned the people in attendance. In the back by the food and drinks stood a familiar face. It was none other than Dick Tripton. He had made it to the wedding. He had a habit of showing up unexpectedly which transferred over from the war. Jimmy was thrilled to see him and they managed to knock down a few beers and have a fantastic time for the remainder of the wedding. It was truly a storybook day for Jimmy and Cindy and they absolutely couldn't wait to get started on building their life and family together. Jimmy had gotten a job working construction in the city and Cindy was working at the Veterans hospital downtown. Still packed with men who came back from the pacific and European theaters in bad shape. She always felt she was indebted to them for their sacrifice, so her work was extremely rewarding to her. They both truly seemed to be living the American dream together. It was all Jimmy had thought about during the war and somedays he couldn't believe that not long ago, he was floating on a raft in shark infested waters in the pacific, wondering if he would ever see Cindy's smile again or hear her laugh. Wondering if he'd ever get the chance to be a husband and a father. He had husband checked off the list and about 6 months after they got married, he was able to check father off the list. Cindy became pregnant with their first child together. He could barely contain his excitement when she told him the news. He hugged her tight and said "I can't wait to watch you be the best mother." As he kissed her on the forehead. "And I can't wait to watch you be the best father." Cindy said sweetly. After the hell Jimmy had survived throughout the war, he, like many other returning solider and sailors finally felt like life was on the right track. There would always be struggles and difficult times, but they were just thankful to have the opportunity to grow old. Many of their friends and fellow Soldiers, Sailors, and Marines would never get that chance. Although he did suffer from survivors' guilt to an extent, and he thought about Ralph and Tom every day,

Jimmy knew they'd want him to make the most out of his life and he planned on doing so by being a good father and husband to Cindy and their baby on the way. Ralph Thomas Katsumoto was born on April 1st 1947. It was a fitting tribute to his friends and the memories they had together. Jimmy and Cindy were now parents to a beautiful baby boy. They'd spend their entire lives together watching their family grow and growing old themselves. Their love was undefinable, as were many relationships of that generation. Built during the tumultuous time of war, it was built to last, and that's exactly what it did.

CONCLUSION

Throughout the war, not only was Jimmy treated unfairly due to his Japanese descent, thousands of other Japanese Americans were treated just as poorly or worse. They were placed in internment camps for fear of being an invasion force. While it may have seemed necessary at the time, after the sneak attack on Pearl Harbor, it tore apart many families. Some who were never reunited. Jimmy had been very lucky to see his father and sister again. The fact of the matter is, this country is built on immigrants and people from other nations who came to America for a better life. They have proven time and time again that they share their loyalty for America and our beliefs. Jimmy fought valiantly in the war to end all wars and survived not just one but two historic moments that will forever be woven into the fabric of our nation. He was willing to fight at all costs for our right to be free. He should have never had to prove himself the way he did to be accepted as a patriot and as someone who loves this country. The fact that he was willing to sign his name on the dotted line to serve at all should have been a testament to his character and his moral compass. He is just one of many examples of men who served that were discriminated against. Soldiers and sailors of

German descent were often labeled as "Nazi's" or "Crouts" or "Hitler lovers" by their peers and had to go through much of the same harsh treatment that Jimmy went through. It just goes to show that during wartime, sometimes we can lose ourselves and who we truly are when placed in a stressful environment where we fear for our way of life. Hopefully valuable lessons were learned from watching how these men conducted themselves when it counted. When their allegiance was tested, they stepped up and came up big for the war effort. Unfortunately, it would be decades before African American military personnel would see the same recognition for their immense sacrifices during armed conflict as well. But the major takeaway is that no matter what color your skin is or where you hail from, if you love this country enough where you are willing to die for it and to protect our way of life and freedoms, you have more than earned the right to be an American and be celebrated for your courage. We are all Americans who bleed the same blood. The same blood our forefathers laid down when they laid out the foundation of our great nation. God Bless the troops and God Bless America.

Dedicated to all those who made the ultimate sacrifice in the European and Pacific Theaters during World War II.